MacFarlane Family
Merry Christmas 2019

Love
the
Obryds

The Sky Farmer

James Oldroyd

illustrations by Rex Amendola

This book is dedicated to Miriam;
your creativity first dreamed of the clouds.

Up before the light of dawn,
Sky Farmer wakes with a yawn.

He begins his daily chores,

opening wide the big barn doors.

Setting up the tallest ladder,
hungry cows begin to chatter.

Up the
ladder
rung by
rung,

into the
sky
his work's
begun.

From starlight
soft as silk,

Mr. Farmer
skims creamy
milk.

Pouring out the Milky Way,
cows sip some milk and eat some hay.

Then clipping at the clear blue dawn,

Mr. Farmer bends to spread the pond.

Snipping at the morning sun,

he drops feathers one by one.

Morning clouds are soft and warm;
they give sheep their woolly form.

When afternoon clouds turn from
white to black,

he cuts horses the patterns they lack.

A rainy spell is good for pigs,
he covers them with long gray wigs.

The rain freezes into ice,
and for the chickens this is nice;

a dozen eggs for their nest,

the hens begin a hatching fest.

When the storm is almost through,

Farmer works to split each hue.

Colors help the garden grow;

fruits and veggies row by row.

And even in his work of haste,

Farmer is careful not to waste.

'Cause a hundred scraps of rainbow light
can turn the flower garden bright.

As Farmer rests at the end of the day,

he watches the sky fade
from bright to gray

Each night while Farmer rests in bed,
the sky replenishes overhead.

In morning, noon and evening light,
in sun and rain and starry night,
Farmer's work in the sky
helps the farm, the earth,
and you and I.

Made in the USA
San Bernardino, CA
23 November 2019